Hello, New House

Jane Smith

CALLIE'S
ROOM
↑UP

Albert Whitman & Company
Chicago, Illinois

For Chris & Phoebe—
home is wherever you are.

Library of Congress Cataloging-in-Publication
data is on file with the publisher.
Text and illustrations copyright © 2020 by Jane Smith
First published in the United States of America in 2020
by Albert Whitman & Company
ISBN 978-0-8075-7226-9 (hardcover)
ISBN 978-0-8075-7228-3 (ebook)

Printed in China
10 9 8 7 6 5 4 3 2 1 WKT 24 23 22 21 20

Design by Theresa Venezia

For more information about Albert Whitman & Company,
visit our website at www.albertwhitman.com.

Sun goes down.

Goodbye, house.

Goodbye, friends.

Goodbye, ocean.

Goodbye, city.

Hello, country.

Hello, new neighborhood.

Hello, new ocean.

Hello, new friend?

Hello, new house.

New living room.

New kitchen.

New bedroom.

Same blankie.

Same bed.

Same toys.

New backyard.

New swing.
Same noise.

New weather.

Worrying weather!

New bathroom.

Same towel.

Same turtle.

Same cup.

Same bedtime.

Same blankie.

Same book.

Same pup.

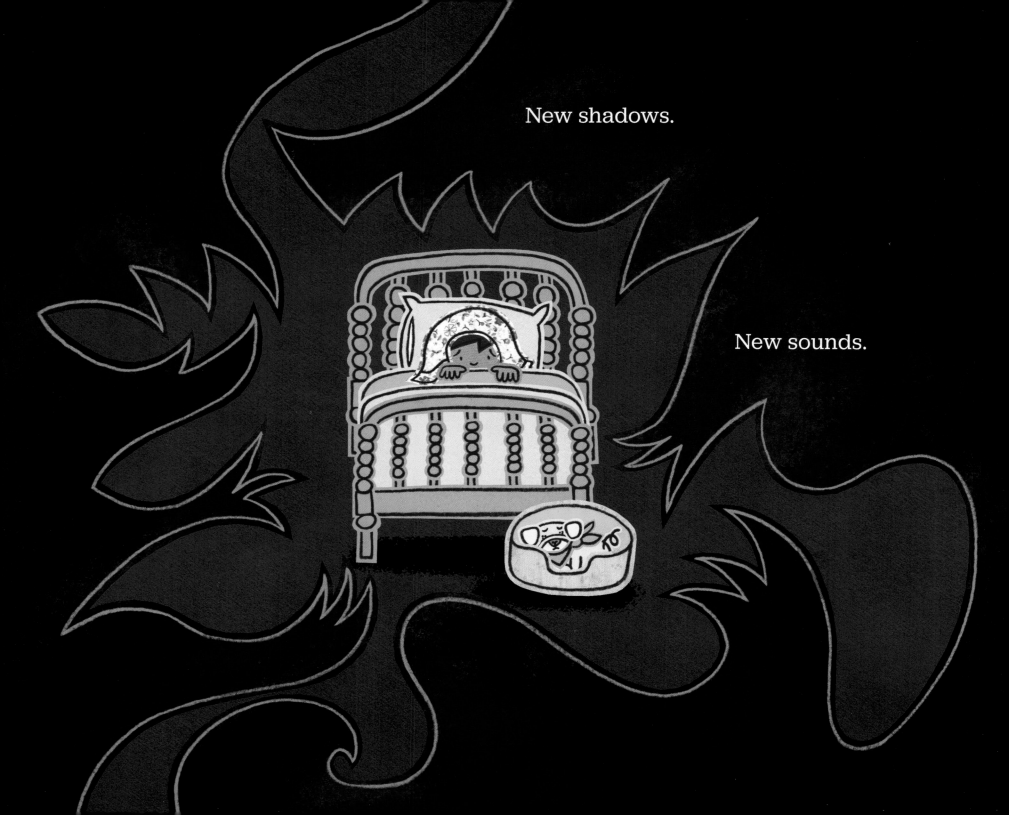

New shadows.

New sounds.

Same Mama. Same Papa.

Same kisses. Same hugs.

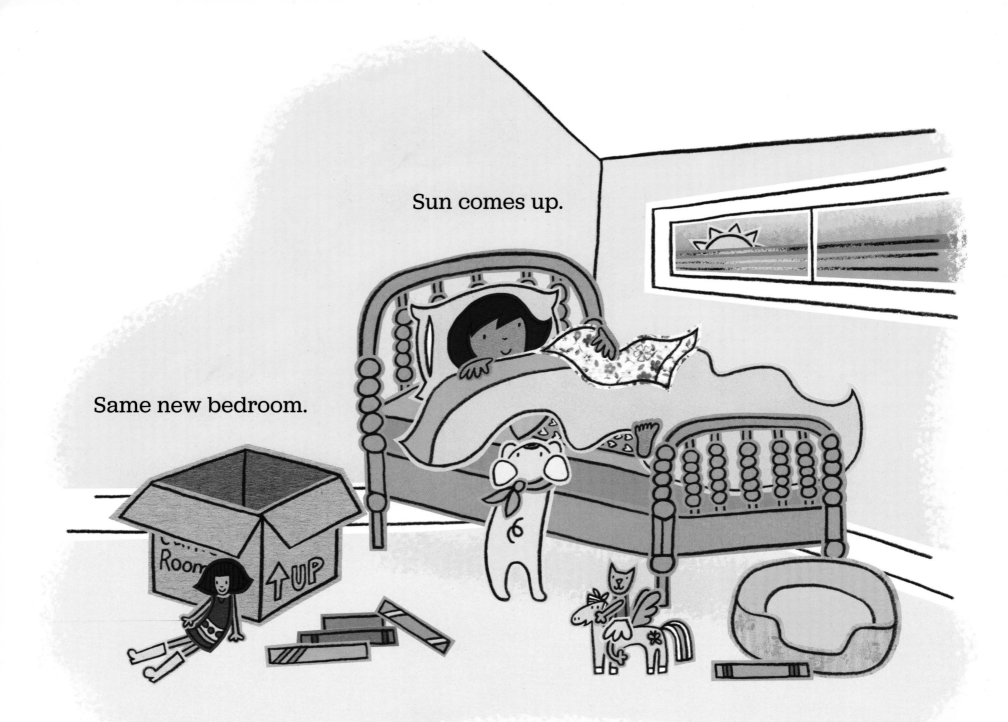

Sun comes up.

Same new bedroom.

Same new kitchen.

Same new house.

Same new backyard.

Same new swing.

Same new friend?

Friends!

Under sun.

Beside ocean.

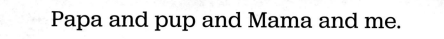

Papa and pup and Mama and me.

Together.

Home.